Beautifully BROWN

By Candice Tavares

NoelleRx
www.NoelleRx.com

Ordering Information:
For details, contact NoelleRx.handmade@gmail.com.

Print ISBN: 978-1-66781-133-8

Printed in the United States of America on SFI Certified paper.

First Edition

Dedicated to brown children all over the globe in hopes that you will always love and appreciate the beautiful brown skin you were born in

♡ Auntie Candice

like coffee or dark chocolate ...

a beautiful

Beautiful

BROWN

like vanilla bean,
café with cream
a beautiful

Beautiful

BROWN

like cinnamon

or gingerbread

a beautiful

Beautiful

BROWN

like ebony

or onyx jewels

a beautiful

Beautiful

BROWN

like caramel
or toffee treats

a beautiful

Beautiful

BROWN

as unique as my fingerprint

a beautiful

Beautiful

BROWN

an olive tan
slighty golden

a beautiful
Beautiful

BROWN

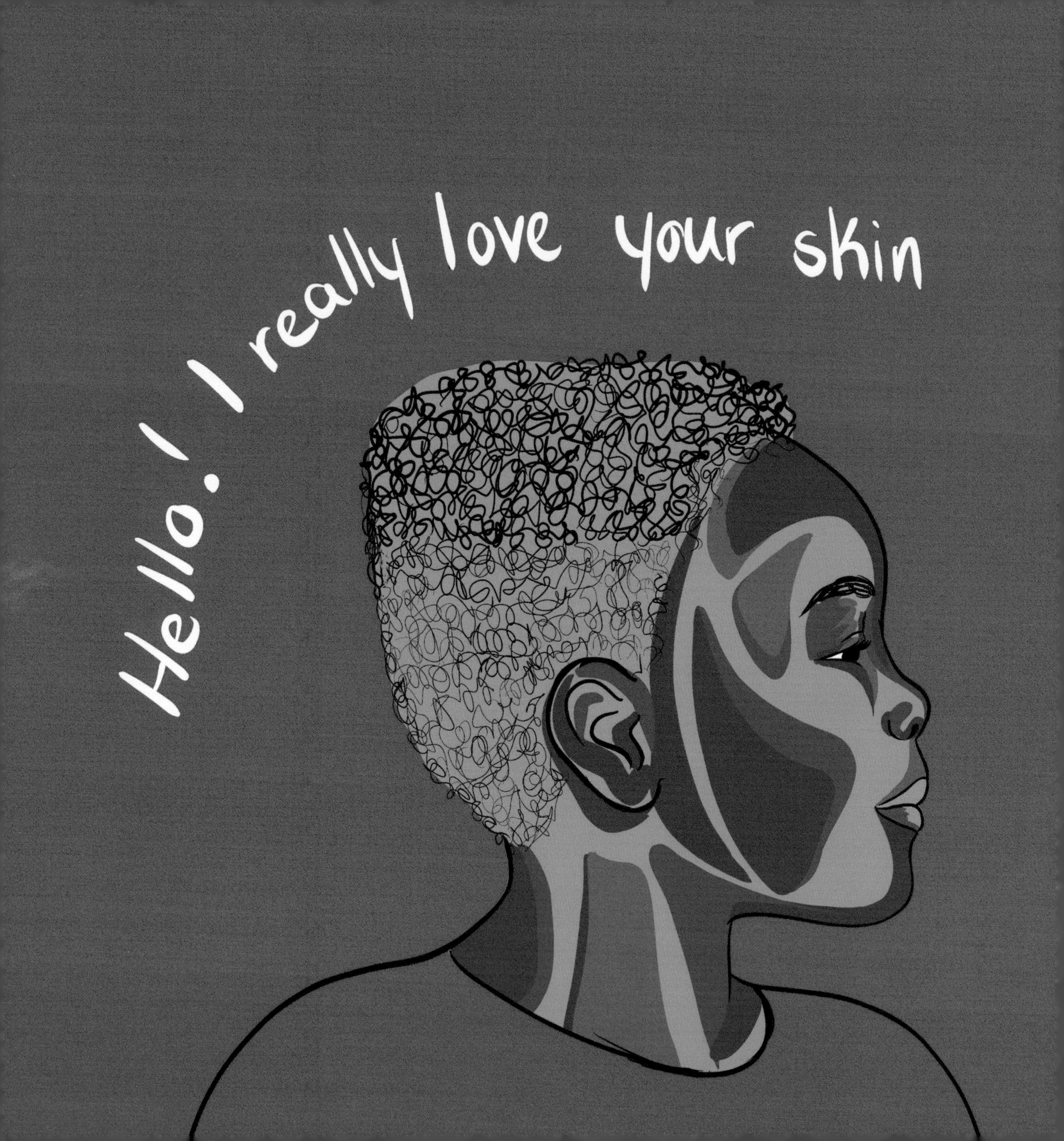
Hello!! I really love your skin

All of us are beautifully BROWN

There is no
need to
compare.

Each shade of brown is equally BEAUTIFUL from very dark to very fair

No matter what

shade of BROWN

you are

you are
BEAUTIFUL
and
perfectly made

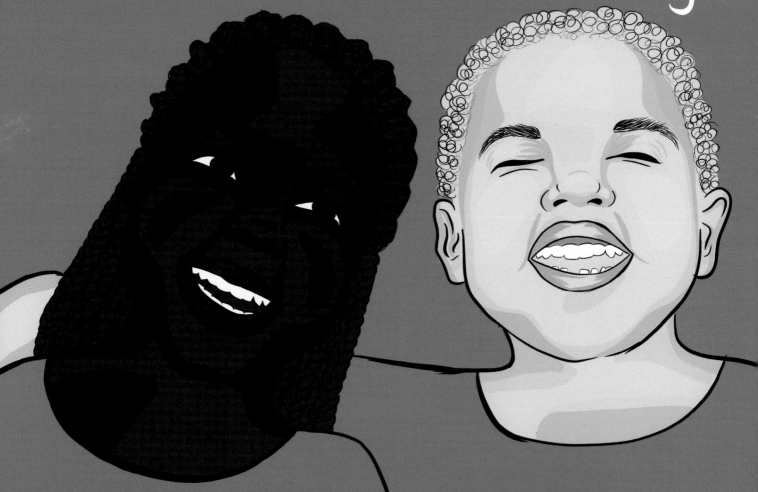

You were made in the

PERFECT

shade!

Your skin is beautifully BROWN too!

Aren't you glad
you were born
in such a
beautifully